ARTIVERSE PUBLICATION
PRESENTS

My Insights

Author
Dr. G. Youveniya

Preface

The journey toward inner clarity often begins in the quiet spaces of the soul, where the clamour of the world fades into a whisper of divine resonance. *My Insights is* a collection of quotes that serves as both a personal testament and a universal invitation to rediscover the "quiet truths" that anchor a life of purpose. Drawing from over seventeen years of experience as an educator and a life rooted in the dual pillars of Faith and Love, Dr. G. Youveniya explores the intricate architecture of human emotion, from the "muscular bond" of companionship to the profound surrender of one's will to the Holy One. This collection does not merely observe life; it interrogates the nature of freedom, the dichotomy of money and morals, and the transformative power of grace, which flows "like dawn spilling gold across the sky". Through these poems, readers are encouraged to navigate their own "inward and outward" journeys, moving away from the muzzles of ignorance toward a life of integration, sanctification, and boundless mercy. It is an offering of peace and humility, crafted for those who seek to find their own "marker" in the vast realm of eternity.

Disclaimer

The poetic reflections contained within *My Insights* represent the deeply personal, spiritual, and philosophical journey of Dr. G. Youveniya. While these verses explore universal themes of faith, morality, and the human condition, they are a heartfelt expression of the author's individual convictions and her devotion to a life guided by humility and grace. Readers are invited to engage with these works as a subjective exploration of inner clarity and quiet truths rather than as a definitive theological or sociological treatise. The interpretations of "truth," "freedom," and "morality" presented herein are reflective of the author's prismatic view of life and her specific spiritual path. Consequently, the publisher and author provide these poems for contemplative and aesthetic purposes, acknowledging that the spiritual experiences and internal realizations described are unique to the author's own "awakening" and may resonate differently with each individual reader.

About the Publication

Welcome to Artiverse Publications — a home where creativity is not measured, ranked, or raced, but respected, nurtured, and celebrated.
Artiverse is more than a publication; it is a metaverse for artists, built by art-lovers who believe that creation deserves empathy, encouragement, and a platform that truly understands its value.

At Artiverse, we do not believe in pitting artists against one another. Our purpose is to uplift, support, and honour every creator's journey. Whether you are an intern learning the craft, a writer finding their voice, an artist experimenting with styles, or a performer expressing through sound—
You are family to us.

To support diverse artistic expressions, Artiverse Publications stands on three strong creative pillars, each playing a vital role in shaping our community
Our aim is to polish writing skills, encourage growth, exchange learning, and build a genuinely accessible literary space for writers across the globe. While we often guide and teach, we believe learning is mutual—many times, we grow through our writers too.

The Word Bond directly connects with Artiverse Publications, as exceptional writers are approached to lead projects, anthologies, and official publications.

It is an open, accessible platform where artists can share, showcase, and shine without fear of judgment. As Artiverse Publications expands, the Artisan's Asylum plays a crucial role in discovering and nurturing visual art that complements storytelling, design, and creative projects.

Further we have An Audio Club that provides a wider exposer to the storytellers, comedians and singers by organising open mics for all

At the core stands Artiverse Publications—the powerhouse that transforms art into opportunity.
It serves as a gateway for creators to publish and earn through their work, ensuring their art reaches readers beyond geographical boundaries. Selected works are officially published on platforms such as Amazon, Flipkart, and Kindle, giving artists the recognition and reach they deserve.

Now that you have a clearer picture of Artiverse as a publication-driven creative metaverse, we are grateful to have you with us. This space will grow stronger, richer, and more meaningful with your creativity, trust, and love.

This is a work of fiction. Names, characters, place, and incidents are either the product of the author's imagination or used fictitiously. Any resemblance to actual persons, living or dead, events, or locales is purely coincidental.

First Edition

Published independently by Artiverse

Acknowledgement

It is my immense pleasure to express my heartfelt gratitude to everyone who supported the creation of this collection. I am deeply grateful to Prakhar (Dev) Agrawal, Founder of Artiverse Publication, and the entire Artiverse team for their expert guidance, professionalism, and encouragement throughout this journey. My sincerest thanks go to my parents, my husband, and my son for being my greatest strength, and to my friends for their unwavering belief in me. Finally, I thank you, the reader, for giving these poems purpose; it is my hope that these verses offer you meaningful moments of reflection and resonate deeply within your heart. Thank you.

Regard,
Dr. Youveniya

About the Book

In My Insights, she records the epiphany moments that illuminate life's journey — moments of clarity that inspire simplicity, humility, and inner strength. Her words are not merely quotations, but distilled reflections born of lived experience and deep contemplation. Through this collection, Dr. Youveniya invites readers to pause, reflect, and awaken to the quiet truths that shape a meaningful life.

About the Founder

He is an emerging writer, motivated by a thoughtful desire to provide healing and support to as many people as possible. His supreme happiness comes from seeing the smiles on the faces of people, he touches with his words, and he's dedicated to inspiring and motivating people in his community to achieve their dreams. He determinedly believes in the power of spreading positivity far and wide. His quotes, stories, and poems draw inspiration from both the real-life experiences of others and the limitless realms of his imagination.

IG - words.bydev

Call - 9179591620

Mail – devkumar120803@gmail.com

About the Author

Dr. G. Youveniya

Dr. G. Youveniya is a devoted teacher and reflective writer with more than 17 years of experience in education. Her life and work are guided by the twin investments of Faith and Love, which she believes are the true wealth of human existence.

Prayer conjugates the humans
with the Divine.

Life is meant to expect the unexpected.

Life: the panoramic luxury of learning.

Love: the height of selflessness.

Patience: the wait for God's timings.

Reactions are heart's instinctive expressions; Responses are minds extrinsic reflections.

Comfort zone is a self-designed curb that limits the potential for vibrant exploration.

Learning is the manifestation of
an intellectual mind.

Life itself is the manifestation of
Divine grace.

The future is never a mystery; in Christ, future is always a victory; that makes a history.

Family, the affective crux of
human life.

Sleep: the taste of death.

Maturity comes with experience,
not just with age.

I wonder! What 'Permanent'
mean in our transient world?

Independence Day: the remembrance of freedom through the ramifications of the nation's partition.

Emotions impregnate life with purpose.

Self-denial is the greatest virtue
of Christian life.

Gratitude is the magnetic virtue
that attracts all other blessings.

Forgiveness, the taintless trail to tranquility of human mind.

Future is the unforeseen fortune o
surprises.

Music, the exhilaration jot to soul.

Christ is the author of
'Forgiveness'.

Every dawn has a dusk, every
start has an end, but in every end,
there is a new beginning.

Teachers are the architects of the future generations.

Memory, the indelible imprint of past in the human mind!

Technology supplants reality with virtuality.

Woman: God's workmanship;
worthy do be praised.

As breathing is to the body, so reading is to the soul.

Moon: the beacon of light – a ray of hope.

Every unfortunateness is a
fortunate flit towards fortitude.

Home: the abode of emotional winsomeness.

Let CHRIST be thy gravitational force in life.

The art of being mindfulness is called ‘Living’ whereas being mindlessness is just mere ‘Existence’.

Motherhood, the celestial bliss of every woman.

Reflections: the minutes recollection of imprints of impression on tranquil mind.

As the moon reflects the light of the sun, so are we to emulate the son – Jesus Christ.

Lust contaminates the soul.

Every minute moment in life is
the very witness of his grace
abound.

Emotions are the intricate web of any relationship.

Teachers trod the untrodden path of knowledge and leave a trail of wisdom.

Travel is the soul rejuvenating experience.

Words are the true adornment of beauty.

Imagination is the innate faculty of human mind.

Forgiveness is the eraser of hurtful stains.

Silence, the language of solitude.

‘FAITH’ is the ‘LIFEBOAT’ in the ‘EARTH’ that saves those abroad, while the earth itself sinks in the ocean of sin.

Flower is an expression of joy.

Giving is the joy of sharing.

Pride, the self-elevated pedestal
of glory built of wax.

Incarnation is the divine in human flesh.

Realization is the awareness of the current state of mind.

Realization is the act of self-exploration.

Tenacity: the deliberate attempt to achieve one's desires.

Depression is the state of failure
succumbed in repetition.

Endurance entices patience into victory.

Drudgery drains the dignity of work.

Abandonment is love undone.

Relinquish: The art of winning by letting go.

Agony is the unsubdued pain.

Carnality is the sensual fire that
burns morals.

Destitute is the stripping of the self from all wealth.

Confession is the acknowledgment of sin for liberation.

Intercession is being the spokesperson towards redemption.

Revelation is the unveiling of the future through the light of eternity.

Penetration is the quiet persistence of Truth seeping into the cracks of resistance.

Atonement is the liberation from
sin clenched life into freedom.

Crucifixion is the curse breaker
for a transformative experience.

Conviction is the sureness of
one's strong belief.

Ambition is the strong wind that sets life's sail in its course of success.

Spontaneity: The unhindered natural flow of thought.

Patience: The willingness to
sustain reality.

Restoration: The act to reinherit one's possession.

Marriage is the eternal
commitment to love.

Home: A Piece of a Place; a place of peace.

Life: An Ephemeral wait for Christ's Second Coming.

Guidance is the Counsel of the wise; to refrain from life's vice.

Like the invisible moon in the
daylight, so are our problems
when God is with us.

Mindfulness: the act of full participation at the moment.

Life is great, not of its extraordinary moments; Life is great in living ordinary moments extraordinary.

Forgiveness is not free; it costs
Christ on the Cross.

Your words season your relationship.

Prayer prevents one from falling prey to errors.

Forgiveness gives life a revival.

Words pierce your soul more than
a sword pierces you.

Every second, minute and hour
are the watchtowers in the ocean
of 'Time'.

Life is an interplay of emotion and reason.

Purity of the soul is possible only
with the divine intervention.

Desire ignites Dreams.

Living is just being in the present.

The divine breath within our body is ‘Life’.

Salvation is the joy of being saved.

Our Savior determines our sanctification.

Nature is God's visible language of Love.

Teaching is the noblest act of knowledge transference.

Love consummates Life.

Purification: The purgation of one's sins.

Purification permeates God's presence in one's life.

Dejection disrupts one's peace of mind.

Dejection is cured with Divine's consolation.

Sacrament is the sacred transaction with the Divine.

Humiliation: The bitter experience of shame and contempt.

Evangelism is the act of echoing Divine's word through human voice.

Tribulations transfixes life's
temptations into transformation.

Sainthood is the triumph of spirit over the self.

Ministry is the embodiment of soul's mission.

Offering is the willing surrender
of the self.

www.ingramcontent.com/pod-product-compliance
Lightning Source LLC
Chambersburg PA
CBHW062143160726
48282CB00027B/917
* 9 7 8 8 1 9 9 7 4 7 9 7 5 *